RED LIGHT DISTRICT

literary art anthology

Edited by
Kerry Cox

Introduction by
Lydia Swartz

Festival Director: Clayton Hibbert

Art Exhibition Director: Sophia Iannicelli

Literary Art Director: Kerry Cox

Literary Art Jurors:

Dobbie Reese Norris

Lydia Swartz

Victor David Sandiego

Eileen Fix

A special thank you to Lydia Swartz for her tireless assistance and support in putting together and editing this anthology.

The Seattle Erotic Art Festival is presented by the Foundation for Sex Positive Culture.

Cover design by Clayton Hibbert

To order additional copies, please visit www.lulu.com

ISBN 978-1-257-76031-2

Acknowledgments

A very special thank you to our 2011 Seattle Erotic Art Festival Literary Jurors: Dobbie Reese Norris, Eileen Fix, Victor David Sandiego, Lydia Swartz and Literary Art Director, Kerry Cox.

In addition, our thanks go to Festival Director, Clayton Hibbert, for his hard work, direction, and cover design.

Also, warm thanks to Art Exhibition Director, Sophia Iannicelli, for walking us through all of the amazing visual and installation art pieces and sharing the stories behind them.

Our deepest gratitude goes to all of the writers who submitted their work - without whom this anthology would not be possible!

Finally, we must thank the Foundation for Sex Positive Culture for putting on the Seattle Erotic Art Festival each year and creating such an amazing showcase for erotic art and the artists who make it.

Contents

Introduction

Everybody writes about sex. The only question is how.

Even people who are not "writers" write about sex. We sext. We leave a note on the bathroom mirror before we sneak out in the morning. We tell stories. We name the parts of our lovers' bodies. We etch dirty pictures on the walls of our caves with rocks or spray paint.

We "writers" write about sex, always. If we claim we don't, we are lying. Let's be honest: A cigar is never just a cigar.

We may leave out the hydraulics and schematics, yet somehow squeeze cum from each word in a passage about horses.

Or, we write in detail about who puts what where when and then what happens, but we're really talking about how we never got over the death of our little brother.

All of the poems and stories the authors generously share with you here expose the soft and hard, sweet and nasty, gauzy and hardcore, coy and raw true facts of life through the lens of the flesh.

***

When you hear one voice singing, it can remind you of your own song. When you hear two voices together, you hear it as a battle or a kitchen where you cook something beautiful. When you hear 20 voices, the sum of their songs is a cathedral – and I don't mean the holy kind; or it could be.

We invite you to hear, to taste. We think you'll find something to succumb to. You know you want to.

Read these words aloud to each other. Get to know the authors and watch for their names and their voices. Let the images and stories invoke your demons, your guardian angels. Let them inspire you. Have fun—and don't forget to write about it.

Lydia Swartz

"At the touch of a lover, everyone becomes a poet."

- *Plato*

Come Lie with Me by Fireside
by E. A. Credgington

Come lie with me by fireside,
Upon this nest of pillows piled high –
In heat that stirs with every flame,
And in the thoughts we entertain.

Come join me in a quiet night,
Delighting in the feelings that we hide,
And fall, as hesitations fade,
To lie within this nest we've made.

A beauty heaven never planned,
I paint your body softly with my hand,
So perfect in its every curve –
A trifle more than I deserve.

In silent gaze, our fears we quell
And hold each other close as passions swell,
For even fire can't disguise
The rhythm of the rain outside.

With every gentile kiss, you shiver,
A secret only eyes deliver –
And rest you then your head upon my chest,
As fire keeps us warm within our nest.

Ashore, again

by Ted D'Leyo

Undo the button on my shirt,
push it back upon my shoulders,
bring near your face and smell my skin,
let the soft hair of my chest
brush your cheeks and lips;
your hands upon my sides.

Trace all within your sight
with fingertips;
from ribs to neck, through chest and arms,
let them disappear beyond sight's edge
to find the depth
of shoulders and of sides.

Then loose what clasps remain
to keep from sight a man's convergent core;
of risen shaft in velvet clad, of crystal dew on crystal thread,
of rounds suspended loose 'midst merging thighs,
in cushioned darkness.

Let hunger prime with want
your lips and breasts,
and the swelling of your throat flow down
to disappear below your heart,
and re-emerge again between your hips;

blooming at the site of your own convergence,
where lips to petals turn, and warmth to nectar,
beneath a pleading, hooded, jewel.

Find the compass of the man
with limbs to guide and draw
velvet shaft to creamy sheath;
kissing never seen but felt
from loin, to breast,
to breathing drawn in rhythmic gasps,
until, convulsing, beg an end,
beyond which lies oblivion,
to lie, thus filled, ashore, again.

Elucidation

by David Jones

she talks like discovery channel
and fucks like animal planet
she makes art that makes me
want to make art
she looks good in the daylight
but sounds better in the dark
she feels good
even when i don't touch her
i'm not safe from her
even in the bathroom
she likes music i've never heard
but can dance to silence
she's too tall for me
to not want to climb
she can almost pick me up
and knows how to take me down
she has her own life
she has secrets that make her unfold
like a flower
and briers as sharp as knives
she's a goddess and a bitch and a woman
all at the same time
she's willing to tell me
what she sees in me
that makes her touch me
of her own volition
she can be blunt and tacky
or classy and discreet as needs be

she'll drink from a bottle
she'll fuck bloody
sometimes she doesn't ask
she just takes
she calls me on my shit
she corrects me when i'm wrong
she tells me to fuck straight off
she tells me to come right over
i don't know
what she's going to do
to, with, for or about me
but i know
it's never happened
before her

Asphalt
by Kyle Jones

The sun was down but I could feel the heat of the day coming up from the asphalt through the thin soles of my Chucks. Carnival sounds reached out from the near distance and we were bathed in the intermittent glow of a blinking fluorescent light stationed a couple of rows away. I'd planned to drop the tail gate and invite her to get off her feet, but she'd wanted none of that.

"There's no time for niceties, Buddy, he'll be out here soon and I need you to fuck me now."

She was like that most of the time, to be honest. When we saw each other, she might greet me with a friendly enough nod, or maybe a "Hey, Buddy" and then slide into the booth with him and his cronies. I'd go back to the kitchen with my bin of dirty dishes and unfinished late night meals and simmer over the way she used me. I wasn't good enough to be her steady, but I was good enough for a quick fuck in the alley behind the cafe when she was horny. He was a good looking, big, strong guy, former captain of the football team, high school big shot and all that, but he didn't get her off. Sometimes I would stare at the back of his head and wonder how he'd react if he realized how much I knew about him. And if he knew how well I knew his girlfriend, well... that'd be cause for a beating, no doubt.

But did I know her, really? I knew the way her pussy felt when she clamped down on my hand at the moment of orgasm. I knew how her mouth tasted: cigarettes and mint gum. I knew the huskiness of her voice when she wanted me to fuck her hard and rough and fast, banging her head against the wall, slamming her hips down against a wooden bench in the park, or pushing her face down against the seat of my truck while I stood outside and fucked her from behind.

That's what she wanted now. The quick, dirty fuck. Her sweet, creamy white ass exposed to the fields beyond the parking lot, my hand buried in her cunt like a hunting dog down a fox hole. I fucked her like it was the last time, like there was no tomorrow, like the last fuck before the world ended.

Because it was the last time.

She didn't know that, of course. I bet it never occurred to her that I'd grow tired of being at her beck and call, dropping whatever I was doing at a moment's notice just because she was too horny to sleep, or study, or think, or breathe. It's fair to ask why it took me so long and I think it's the same way you can keep smoking long after you know how bad it is for you. It's a habit, it's what you know, it's easy and your friends expect to see you with that smoke hanging off your lips. She expected me to be there, to offer a 'helping hand' as she'd say, and for a long time I had been. Even if it chapped my ass to see her strutting around on the arm of that Neanderthal, I didn't have the guts to ask for more. Or maybe — and this is the realization that had been growing steadily — maybe I knew all along she wasn't worth that kind of effort.

Easier to leave. Leave this stupid, fucking, dead-end town. Leave this dead-end job. Leave behind the backwards, backwoods mental deficiencies of everyone who lived here and treated me like dirt. I'd finally made my peace with the fact that she was never gonna leave him for me. Hot sex under a street light wasn't enough to keep me here. I'd already packed my gear, and cashed my last paycheck.

I have to say, I enjoyed fucking her that night. The swirl of noise from the carnival sounded like a John Waters movie soundtrack. Forever more, the smell of popcorn, cotton candy and the acrid odor of cooling asphalt will take me back to that moment: her face pressed against the rough fabric of my seat cover, her shorts around her ankles, the wet sounds of my fist in her pussy, her harsh panting breaths lengthening into the growling moan that meant she was about to come. I finished her off and pulled out. She groaned and struggled to get her breath. Sometimes she'd offer to return the favor, but I knew it wouldn't happen tonight, not with him and his friends so close by. And, really, I was OK with that, I could get myself off.

"Damn, Buddy, that was so good." She leaned against me, pressing me against the door frame, momentarily soft and yielding and affectionate. I pulled her in tight, got a handful of hair and pulled her lips to mine. The kiss was deep, my tongue gave no quarter, briefly, she was all mine. She gave in to me, sighing against my mouth and for a moment, indecision hovered in my mind. *Damn*, I thought, *I'm gonna miss this.*

And I suppose I will, but there's plenty I won't miss, and that's what I focused on as I drove out of town that night. It would have been easy to stay, to stay on as her fuck buddy, her occasional sex toy, but I needed more out of life. The occasional fuck, no matter how good, would never make up for the way she didn't see me most of the time. It wasn't enough to keep me in a town where most people didn't see me and, when they did, it was usually with a sneer or a look of pity.

I rolled the window down, sticking my elbow into the warm night air. The radio was cranked up and I pressed down on the accelerator, pushing my old truck as hard as she could go. The road was empty for the time being and I needed to put some quick distance between me and my past. The moon was full, shining benevolently down on the miles of asphalt ahead of me and the growing number behind, and as I thought about my destination, my heart rate went up and currents of adrenaline and anticipation ran through my body. The longer I drove, the more sure I was about my decision. I grinned as one of my favorite Garth Brooks songs came on. I sang out loud to the moon as my truck drove me toward the rest of my life.

Ain't going down 'til the sun comes up

Ain't givin' in 'til I get enough

Going 'round the world in a pickup truck…..

Ain't going down 'til the sun comes up

(no) strings attached

By Charai Dela

i am always surprised at
how easily i can go back
in my mind

how easily you pick me up
my heart
on the point of a needle
not like the butterfly
(one being's death for another's curiosity)
but still beating
its wings
and all the more vivid for your inspection

how easily we thread
these salty beads on a twine
of desires called forth and answered

you tug at my heartstrings

there is a warm ocean within me
and it's breaking through the surface
of my skin

Entre Chien et Loup
by Aurora Day

I saw your beast
There, in the magic in-between
Of summer sun and endless night.
As your eyes flickered with long hunger
And your sharp teeth smiled with powerful need—
Purple heat surged from the earth
Upwards to my cunt.
Swollen, sudden need. Wet fire.

You grabbed my arm, silently
Bidding I rise.
And dragged me to the wooded grove.
Stripped me bare.
Saw every darkness in me.

The air around us hummed "yes"
As your beast suckled my breasts.
My coiled ache rose, and rose
Consuming my flesh until
It sprang forth in naked freedom
Unashamed ecstasy. Yours.

You entered me quickly, stiff cock
Plunging deep into my flesh,
A dagger of lust splitting me open
   Body and soul.
      Oh. And OHHHHHH.

Growling moans rising
   With the moon
      Ahhh. And AHHHHHH.
Until you came, shuddering,
   Trembling
Your eyes entwined in mine
As we welcomed the stars.

happy easter
by Layla Tromble

so let me get this straight
we had this goddess right
mother who was messy with passion
and anger and sadness and sex and jizz and
joy and bliss
she was actually worshipped because of the power
of her heart and her pussy and her sword and her plow
depending on which face you looked into
men and women both prayed & sacrificed & fucked
in her name and to exalt the divine within themselves and their lovers
she was powerful and draped in blue
and then someone somewhere decided all those things were too much of a threat
so they let her keep the blue robes but
took away the mess they cleaned her up gave her one face
with doe eyed innocence and blissful subservience
to this angry punishing father god they sealed
up her cunt, made her immaculate
the mother who didn't even have
to fuck god to get knocked up
she just had to be quiet and accepting
no fighting, no passion, and certainly no jizz
not hers or anyone else's
and whole generations were raised to fear their own passion
distrust the fact that fucking feels way better than taking communion
and certainly brings you closer to god
there is divine energy in pleasure and pain
you can't convince me the only reason those priests flog themselves
is to prove penitence
i know what that pain feels like and it may bring me closer to god
but not because i feel like shit for taking it
it's about damn time to throw off the blue robes that have been used
to cloak the body of the divine in guilt & shame and
fucking let mother mary finally get laid again

when you fuck and you yell out for god it's not blasphemy
it is worship it is praise it is a prayer to a
goddess we've tried to forget
but somehow way back in some cultural memory
we never surrendered
so be messy with passion and anger and pain and pleasure
and blood and jizz and joy and bliss
and send up a prayer of thanks whenever
your pussy is wet
or your dick is hard
and open yourself to the connection that only comes
from the release of energy the cosmic fucking heat & bliss
of messy, dirty, naughty, sinful, holy, sacred
sex.

In the House Where You Live

by Raina Johnson

The evening sun was dull as we walked up the stairs
to the old house that you lived in
with your girlfriend
and her son.
I could see my shadow outlined on your broad back
and I took comfort in knowing
I was already
on you.
The door was open when we arrived as though it knew to
expect us early from dinner
where your hand
worked its way
steadfastly, first on my ass then to the front of me....
I did not scold,
nor fright
at the boldness of your fingers that seemed to assume
my openness
willingly,
nor did I feign any thrill that you saw,
smelled,
felt
or tasted
as you finally entered me.
As you led me upstairs and took off the last bit of my
hesitation
and wore me like a kid's glove,
I saw how the sun shone through the Victorian oval window.
It cast its canary
yellow glow
across your shoulder blades where I saw each freckle and
imperfection
and I cut my teeth
like an infant,
on your
bicep,

ignoring blemishes,
pushing aside the who and what and where,
and welcoming only the primordial custom that we renewed here
in the house
where you live
with your girlfriend
and her son.

I Will Wait
by Tom Nivison

I wait for you
On knife edge
Near the end of night.
I wait for you
In a stiff wind
At a bus stop
Or your front step.
I wait for you
While rain swells
And surges thru the streets
Under a dark umbrella.
I wait for you
With the engine running
And the radio wailing
Your favorite song.
I wait for you
Thru snowblind moments
Of horizontal madness.
I will wait til you come.

All My Red Roses
by Charai Dela

My pain is a little black bird
in the cage of my heart
In a crimson chamber
I hide in the furthest corner
my need, my want, my longing
Scarlet darkness
red, hot, deep

You tie me down
with love
I struggle, desperate
world turned upside down
chains turned inside out
made manifest

I resist you
You resist
my crying, begging, fighting
you hold me down
lift me up

I surrender
I give up, give in
I go down
falling
deeper, deeper
into myself

You catch me
hands at my innermost door
and blindfolded I dance
feeling I see
I become skin, flesh, bone
deeper, deeper

You open me
tender and hard
feathers and whips
rose petals and thorns

And opened I bleed
skin weeping tears
sweating precious pearls
From a dozen wounds
I flow heartblood-red
pulsating, thrashing
moaning, sighing

Wings fluttering I escape
You set me free, break down my walls
I break free from myself
I become more
Growing into one-ness
I transform
pain into pleasure
weakness into strength
hurt into healing

Hidden chambers
bathed in alchemical gold

In the Dark

by Maureen Betita

In the
dark
of that
cell
I felt
your
hunger

I longed
to
fulfill
it

To fill
your
mouth
with
me.
Slide
down
your
throat
and see
your
thirst
slaked.

Your hot
breath
on my
skin
at my
throat
left me
wet

In the
dark
I
would
have
welcomed
you.

shame #1

by Jen Cross

When I say I want to let you into my shame, this is what I mean: I want you to shove all the stories back in my face sometimes. I want us to be honorable with one another, I mean, I want us this mean and broken. It's too scarce and I don't know for sure how I'm going to get in it, but this is what I imagine:

She's in a hot room and it's quiet and it's late and there's no traffic noise outside. Inside, her body is thickened warm with ignominy and she is naked up against the headboard and the bedclothes are cheap and worn and, as yet, unmussed. She maybe has her clothes somewhat open — her shirt unbuttoned, her pants unzipped, her shoes off. This is how she always used to be. You are clothed here in this hotel room. You sit on a cheap sturdy pine wood chair at a desk that has on its surface a notepad and a white plastic pen and a molded plastic dark translucent tray holding two plastic-encased water cups and a fraudulent empty ice bucket. You are drinking good whisky from one of the glass water cups out of the bathroom. There is one light in the room, the awkward bulb drowsed beneath a white frosted gold gilt shade, and it's on over her head, and all the shadows in the room are rough and stark. It's a long time since it was midnight and you and she are both turned on and she is terrified and you aren't sure if you shouldn't be, too.

But you have been here before. You are familiar with the rough pearly caress of humiliation. You've had her telling you stories all night, stories about what her father did and how, what her uncle did and where, how old she was and what her body felt like. You are trying to get all the answers, not because you're trying to turn her or yourself on with the memories. You want to know where the flint still burns her, and you watch how and when her eyes cast down to the bed when she describes how her cousin watched once, when her uncle made her take his cock in her hand and work it quick and callous 'til he shot in her face, and that she locked eyes with her cousin, who was an older girl and pretty, and felt emboldened and powerful at what her cousin's daddy was having her do. She hasn't yet learned, figured, how to rip that power from her skin, you see, or if she should. You want to use that.

When you ask her to touch herself, to slip her two clean hands beneath the denim and zipper, beneath the flowered cotton panties, you'll make her tell you how proud she was when she knew more about fucking than any of her boyfriends, how she led them to her body like cattle, let them feed there because they were soft and rugged and fawn-eyed and easy to maneuver around. You'll make her tell you what else she wanted from that cousin, even for an instant, 'cause at 11 the body doesn't know much beyond what could keep it feeling good and tingly, and there was at least something in every one of those terrible instances that rang tingly through her legs, her belly, her cunt: those were the parts   the wounds   that never closed. You will open her further—partner in bleeding it back out—you will ask her for her shame while she comes.

Lions of Summer

by Tito Titus

The lions were at the beach
again today, not roaming
but resting in the homeless man's shelter
beneath a blue tarp stretched
over bales of hay.
They were peaceful, yawning and napping
with the old bearded man.
            I wondered what he feeds to them
            as I hurried past.

Across the street, a man and woman sunbathed
naked in a vacant lot strewn
with industrial debris, rusted hulks
of refrigerators and trucks.
The woman lying on gunnysack piles
arched her back as if to touch the sky
with her well oiled and full breasts.
The man noticed nothing
except the bouncing magazine in his lap.
            I wondered what he reads to her
            as I sauntered past.

Perspective
by Ted D'Leyo

Quite near
an Orchid blooms
amidst the heather
its scent filling my senses

Beyond it
and across the plain
the hills of Anu rise
softened by the distance

On the far horizon
the goddess' face reclines in mist
lips parted
at the blooming
of the Orchid

Authors Note: Being terribly near sighted myself, to my unaided eye very little distance reduces clarity as a very great distance normally would. The "Paps of Anu" are a pair of matched hills in County Kerry, Ireland, thought to be the breasts of the goddess "Danu."

TALES OF MONTANA

1900, May 29

Dead Piegan Creek
by Jae Carlsson

i

His hands reach right through your skin and course along bare muscle fiber. You ache. You want to gasp but swallow it in a shudder. The prongs of his fingers skid unmercifully along the strands of your sinew, up the long muscles of your legs, up the flat muscles that flank your torso, in a bald scuttle across armpits, in fissures down your back, across and over, and on and on, stretching you in every direction, stretching you 'til the only self-awareness you have is of an endless unrelenting furrow. You shake uncontrollably. You forget who you are and where you are, and the only thing that you remember is who you are with.

ii

Summer has blown in, hot, dry and dusty. You smell cattle in the wind. The canvas shutter covering your window flops about in the breeze. You nonchalantly rotate your body onto your stomach. Spines of light knife their way across your room and disappear. Darcy is no longer in bed.

Your cheek is lazily flat to the mattress as you peer into the darkish room. You locate him sitting atop your clothes chest, finishing dressing. When done, he gazes back at you with such cool discernment that it penetrates your pores. Goosebumps rise all over.

> What do you see when you look at me like that?

> I don't know...,

he says, pausing to think. He enjoys a long silence, then rolls out the words slowly.

> You are a tawny girl, sleek and sinuous. But with smooth moist skin, darkened by sweat and the sun. Not rounded and rosy and soft enough, perhaps, for the average man's taste, but it is very much what I favor.

Contemplating some more, he chooses his words carefully, like he were writing it in, or reciting it from, a diary.

> Your face, never cheerful, is shadowed like Dead Piegan Creek where it glides through the cottonwoods. Yet it is like cooling embers, glistening somewhere deep underneath.

You feel a wave of warmth inside but don't move a muscle. This must be poetry, like you've read about in stories. You are thrilled that someone would take the trouble to talk about you this way. However, you are not one to be overawed by compliments, or to foolishly display how words make you feel.

> You must be a college-educated man.

> Stanford.

You pull yourself off the bed and hunt up some riding clothes.

> So what do you think this new century is going to bring?

iii

Up the draw, up from the Piegan Creek settlement you ride, onto the high meadows. Together with him, but apart. Together only in the landscape you share.

Reining his horse to a stop, he points up the gorge to where it cuts through the escarpment and decides that this must be the extreme edge of the property. Still a man in his twenties, Darcy was hired just this year to manage the Palmera spread. A vast estate, it stretches from Piegan Creek, the north boundary, southward clear to the county line, and up from near the railhead into the foothills. The main ranchhouse, one of twelve, is way down outside of Dawson.

You're married, right?

Two years,

he says, unperturbed.

Must be hard on her. I hear you spend a lot of time on the range.

You hear right.

He pulls his horse away and canters into the trees.

What you hear is that he is conscientious. Particularly now, getting to know new territory and acquainting himself with his drovers out at these far stations. Trying to learn all he can before the autumn roundups and the first snows. Driving two steers ahead of him, he emerges from the trees further down. You gallop to join him. But till sunset, he is a man lost in his work.

You bed in a windless hollow near the trees.

In the morning he will head south, you back to Piegan.

I like my wife,

he volunteers, without prompting,

just as I like civilized values. But I have to admit that I like the range too, a lot. I like the wind and open spaces and feel beneath me of horse's hooves churning through the tall grass; to wake up cold in the morning and be brought back to life by the heat of the rising sun. To piss at the sky.

You fling a couple pebbles into the fire, sending up sparks.

Darcy, you'll be getting back this way?

A day or two, likely every third week.

That Sort of Thing
by Raina Johnson

Boot heels never did much for me
until your father walked in, and I saw his....
I don't mean any disrespect,
you understand,
But he doesn't really even try to hide
the all too familiar signs
and symbols
Etched into his flesh,
Dangling from his neck,
And you know how I always loved
That sort of thing.
My heart pounds when he raises his hand
towards my face,
and spittle flies from his mouth,
into mine.
Oh, and there was that time,
When he commented on my very ethnic nose
and said something about Jesus and a terrible crime.
I kind of feigned fright
and fidgeted furiously
while he preached and scolded me and then
he stepped on my fingers
And broke
each
one
of them:
I heard them crack; I saw them turn blue, like his eyes.
The fingers curl under now,
so I sit here, in front of him and use my knuckles
to play with the pleats in my skirt,
while he reads to me from The Book.
Your father
is a fantasy of mine.
I feel like maybe you should know why
He keeps me
Locked tightly in the basement,
where I am safely reserved, just for him.

I listen carefully to the creak and clunk
of his boots on the floorboards:
I like to hear him coming,
the sweat forms,
my fingers remember,
my body remembers,
my mind cries, "yes, oh, yes."

When We're Dangerous Like This
by Roxy Jones

It's that way that he — daaamn — leans against that wall, looking like a fight just desperate to jump ya with his button fly jeans, old friends that know how to hug him just right, with that grease stain on the side that reminds me where his mind likes to stay and his no big deal hair that you know took him hours in the mirror to learn to comb just right, so he can pull it off fast and easy when the pretty girls are watching, and he stares like a bull, like a prayer on fire, with those eyes — god, those eyes, coke-bottle green, with a wink that tells you things your mama never did — and he stares right through me, yeah me, like I'm meat and he's the hungriest man on earth and you know he'd rip right through you... yeah, he loves me right then like leather loves soul, like a man loves a woman when she's down on her knees on the ground but he loves her like lace, and he holds her like

a loaded weapon.

Yeah, that's the way my man waits for me while I pull on the lace and the beads and the so-red-he-should've-crossed-himself-twice-before-kissing-me lipstick that makes him go weak in the knees and wild inside, and I walk right by him, so close he can smell roses and sex and hairspray, that smell that says "I look this way for you, boy, so you better take notice" with a dip that lets him see how good I taste and he knows how lost I am in his low gravel voice and his slick cowboy boots and his I-couldn't-care-less-arms that care so hard they nearly rip me in two. With my heels clicking hard on the wet asphalt and my scent wrapped around his mind like my fingers in his hair we dance together, a slow, sexy walk, a challenge to the night to be darker than we are, dark and hard like the creatures that hide in the shadows of the street and make nice folks want to lock their doors and hide away from lives that scream and howl with passion and greed, those sexy wonderful nights when

we're dangerous like this.

The Girl With Tears in Her Eyes

by Kimberlykate Neagle

It is the crack of the whip
that tears open the night
and spills stars across the sky.
Then even the gods
will turn their heads
from the girl
with tears in her eyes.

It is the weight of the stroke
that pulls down the moon
and shifts the evening tide.
Time will stand still
and bend to his will
for the girl
with tears in her eyes

It is the strength of his hand
that tames the tempest
until still the river lies.
Courted by wind
His favorite sin,
the girl
with the tears in her eyes.

Deeper
by Evoë Thorne

I struggle because I like the feel of the fight.
Show me your strength, Baby.
Prove that you are worthy of my surrender.
Bind me to your will.
Hold me fast,
And you'll know when you hold my heart.

Open my eyes.
Show me Innana's footsteps in the dust of my soul,
Lead me deeper.
I'll dance naked to your drum.
Take me down
To the simple beat of leather on flesh,
To a rhythm of sensation.
Breath in, breath out.
I want to feel you
In the throb of every heartbeat
And the sting of every stroke.
The only path to peace I know is pain.

Open me up with your heat
Petal by petal like a dewy rose
In the bright light of a summer morning.
Strip me bare.
Make me scream.
Baby, the only refuge I need,
Is you.

Give me waves,
Deep oceanic currents,
To crest and ride above the swirling debris of my mind
And crash against the rocky shores.
Let me break against the force of you,
Then draw me in with your undertow.
Take me deeper.

Open the door
To the quiet places inside.
Show me your world,
Knowing beyond words
The mysteries of you.
Make us one.

When I am breathless and begging,
Burning with desire,
Dionysus shivering and shattered,
Baby, let me be your temple
And your tempest.
Enter and find haven in the circle of my arms.
Let me rock you over and over
'Til the storm subsides.

And then I'll take you deeper...

home: again
by Jen Cross

The first time I laid my hand all the way inside another woman was revelatory. This experience of being contained in a body, being allowed in, is that what it was? How, when I slid my hand up into her, I finally got what was so interesting to all those boys for so many years, even if I hadn't known I was wondering: having something of themselves centered and whole and engulfed in someone else's flesh. This kind of penetration wasn't anything I'd ever been trained to do, wasn't something that media or locker room stories had even conditioned me to want: this me, pushing, rocking slow persistent response to her joy, this woman who let me go there in her, who took pleasure always as sort of her due, I mean, she opened up to her longing and sex like there was never going to be anything hidden in it to scare her, or scar.

She turned her dark-furred self inside out for me, and I was aghast at so much trust, the way her cunt just continued to open, sluicing out fluid, and I sloshed myself with more lube and teased her with the thickest parts of my palm, the parts of me that can do such a thing as penetrate, and then the ribs of her muscles crowed around the bulk of my hand: the ball beneath my thumb, the knobs of my knuckles. One more sharp urge, and that pop, the sudden, plain, extraordinary: *Oh God, I'm in!*

And then she'd come hard and vice-gripped around me, and nothing else is moving, nothing but the full flush of her contractions. I remained frozen 'til she cooled just a hinge, started sneaking open and I could slowly slick and slide sweat and spit and lube around where her skin had suctioned to mine, ricocheting after-shocks through her thighs 'til I was out.

And what about receiving? Taking someone's fist dear god: no biocock just now riding quick to friction and then to come when I was just barely beginning to enjoy the ride, this could go on for an hour, more, her sliding out and popping home again

home again

in me and open all that thick and wide and perfect for a size queen, an hour of how. fast. can. you. make. that. arm. go. Tiring shoulders, forearms, biceps, back: taking, taking, taking. And when the crest came, for me, there was no straight serious clutching orgasm, this ride was altogether into the face of my grief: fisting fucked me into sobbing sorrow and my lover had to figure a way to hold me with her free arm, the other fitted still and quiet against my cervix ('cause I wouldn't let her move) as rage and shame wailed hard in waves, thick and through and out of me   and then that magic   how can I tell you?

the release when I could breathe again, the world wet and blurry around my peripheral vision, one more layer of terror sloughed off   and oh, there she is   moving in me again   just shifting but the heat stood to roll and boil through me and I said   OK

and she said   You sure? And I said   I think I said

I moved down hard onto her   I said   Yes, Yes

then shoved up and back and down on her hand, and yes

on her hand, all the way in me, until the luscious howling crowded out the horror that so often shadowed us, until the smell of pussy and work and grown lust was the only thing filling our room again.

His First Massage

by Tracy Lee

Face down
On the table
He lies
Naked
Oil on my hands
I knead his shoulders
Continue down his back
Another pair of hands appears
We each take a side
Rubbing
Caressing
Enjoying the touch
Treating this man to pleasure
I take over
Climb on the table
Up his legs
Straddling him
His tailbone my seat
Wearing nothing but slippers
I oil my breasts
Lean over him
Whisper in his ear
Slide my body down his

Full contact
No-hands massage
What fun
Playtime for the masseuse
It gets better…
Time for him
To roll over

Conjure the Wind

by Maureen Betita

Let us conjure
some wind
love.
Wind to fill
our sails
speed us to
safety.
As we test
the strength
of our
magic.
Enter my
circle
with passion
alert.
As I call the
quarters,
your heat
at my back.
The sea
beneath us
senses our
frisson.
The deck
stretches to
our groans.

Ride me gently
as I reach
for the air,
stir the
elements to
respond to
my need.
I feel you
inside me
deep as the
sea.

Pressed to
your chest
we kneel
in the circle.
Your hands
at my breasts
your breath
on my neck.
Together we
call to the
wind
Your strength
matching
mine.
Intent to
intention.

Our magic
rises to
answer.
Thrust answers
thrust.
I am lost to
your
swordplay
as the wind
fills our
sails.

I cry sometimes
by Layla Tromble

i cry sometimes when you touch me
not because i am sad
but because i feel the touch of your
hand not just on my skin
or in my wet cunt
but because i feel
your strong delicate artistic
fingers
somewhere deeper
wrapping themselves around
my scarred sometimes scared
sacred heart
because the feeling of your hand there
reminds me of the strength
with which it beats
the power that resides there amid
the blood and memories
and hopes and dreams
between the words that define it
and the iron that feeds it
your hands come there with
heavy beauty and leave their marks
fingerprints deep red whorls
not just in slippery red but dark
indelible on muscle that has worked
to learn to love and accept
and remain tireless in its beating
i cry sometimes when you touch me
not just from the release or the feeling of your hand
on my flesh
but from the feeling of your fingers that could crush
but instead hold safe delicate power

Silent Seduction

by E. A. Credgington

An absence of words, a moment in time,
Lost between love and the lust on your mind,
Caught in a lingering longing subdued
By the thought of your body, an elegant nude —
And the call of our passions, our souls intertwined
To play on the playground of thoughts in your mind,
Enraptured to capture the heat of your touch
That sends my heart spinning in physical rush —
And I blush for a moment, defining the cause
Of a time without words as our passions give pause.

Abstinence

by C. C. Havens

I am wet with desire.

My mouth salivates at the sight of my back country skier sitting beside me. It's not the sexy hint of silver at his temples or the hardness of his chest straining against his polypropylene shirt. I'm not craving his lips, his tongue, his cock.

I am lusting after his grilled cheese sandwich.

I swallow hard as he takes the first bite. As his teeth penetrate the thick sprouted-wheat bread, I hear the soft crunch of the buttery grilled crust. I squirm in my wood chair as the cheese stretches out from his lips. I imagine leaning over, sucking the strand of chewy mozzarella into my mouth and letting it seduce me back to all that bready bliss.

But I don't.

I scrape the last spoonful of my lentil brown rice soup into my mouth and try to distract myself with the bowl of fruit on the kitchen table. This tactic lasts about five seconds. My gaze gravitates back to my man's plate, lured by the heady aroma of warm buttery bread.

It's a classic case of the lure of the forbidden. Some women secretly lust after their best friend's teenage son. Others fantasize about seducing their married co-worker. For me, it's bread.

I haven't had wheat in three months. No chewy toasted bagels lathered in cream cheese. No dense pumpernickel warm out of the oven saturated with butter. Why?

After catching every cold that infiltrated my small mountain community the past two years, I decided to go on a mission to strengthen my immune system. Coincidentally, an old friend called the next day and spoke of his mother-in-law and her determination to fight cancer. A naturopathic doctor suggested that she quit eating refined sugar and wheat to strengthen her immune system after the devastation of chemotherapy. Like a good hypoglycemic, I'd already cut most of the sugar from my diet years ago and the idea of eliminating wheat sounded intriguing. I decided to try it.

Unfortunately, it's working. While my friends and yoga students suffer with various colds, flues and viruses, I've been immune. Not even a sniffle.

I can't quit now.

But my resolve is crumbling like a blueberry muffin. Abstinence isn't my forte. But neither is coughing up green phlegm. It's simply a choice. Well, maybe not that simple.

Right now I want those two pieces of golden brown bread wrapped around all that oozing cheese more than anything. We climbed over 4000 vertical feet on our telemark skis today. I deserve it. My dinner of soup and rye crackers is long gone and feels like air inside my belly.

My skier's sandwich is almost a memory. He eats it fast, mechanically, as if it wasn't the most amazing thing in the world. To him it is just fuel. If it was mine, I would chew slowly, savoring and cherishing it like a final kiss from a lover at the airport. I seriously consider reaching over and snatching the last bite.

But I don't.

I grab the apple from the bowl of fruit as he pops the last bit of crust into his mouth and licks his fingers. Feeling a pang of grief for my unfulfilled hedonistic self, I bite ravenously into the apple, a bite so big that the sweet juices overflow and dribble down my chin. He swallows and stares greedily at me.

“That looks good,” he says as he leans forward, licks the juice from my chin, and reaches for my apple. My hand snaps back. I am not sharing.

The apple is extended far behind me as our lips meet. I taste the earthy glutinous wheat, the thick oils of the butter and cheese on his lips. Suddenly, I want to devour him. I kiss and lick all around his lips that are slick, salty and reminiscent of yeast. My tongue dives deep into his mouth, hungry for more.

His arms, much longer than mine, get the apple. He licks the juices off the exposed, pale flesh and kisses me again. Our tongues dance, a tango of tastes: wheat, sweet, buttery, juicy. My tongue slides down his neck exploring the saltiness of his skin from our day of exertion. I grab the apple, rub it down his neck and lick slowly, from his collarbone to his ear, savoring every inch of his sweet, salty taste. He takes the apple from me and tosses it on the table.

He pulls my fleece sweater over my head, releasing my hair from its ponytail and guides me towards the bear-skin rug in front of the woodstove.

It's time for dessert. The sweetest kind.

Lust at Sea

by Marie Freulon

Each time I try to forget, there is always something you say that keeps me tuned into you. A daily reminder. A social network.

How did your physical changes got to turn me on even more than before?

That day, that photography you uploaded, had nothing to do with any other ones I had seen. The ones I fell in love with, weeks ago.

You had undergone a massive change.

You, with the half-mooned, black bags under your eyes. Your short mohawk hair in a mess, under your hooded sweatshirt. Your pear-shaped face almost angulated in an 'I give up' type of look. No trace of any make-up. Not much left of that feminine touch that showed up on all your previous pictures.

It was over between us. Nothing had even really started. Sweet words. That feeling of elevation, when someone shows interest in you. Comfort to comfort. I believed in us like a kid believes in Santa Claus. Focusing on you so hard, no other woman would appeal to me. Still I was drawn to all the womanhood in you right there. Things you see beneath the surface. Feelings you get past a certain degree of liking someone. That photo of you, turned me on immediately. I wanted you right then. I wanted you to crave me too. To step out of that image, and be with me. Joined together in long lasting heretic love. The type we could have been burned for at that age of witches. Nothing muted, nothing silenced. A disgrace to the holy; a rejoice to the devil. Things you had said to me days before, forced that feeling deeper. How much I wanted you to come at me, and put your words to execution. You could have done anything you wished, and it would have pleased me as well. I would have been your devotee.

Your accentuated tired features, digging my neck. Your hands doing justice to my flesh for that long time overdue. Your filiform, bony figure, running on mine like a snake slides easily through, like he knows what he's doing.

Your generous lips hovering over each bump of my body, like a sacred temple to explore.

Milky flesh versus toffee skin. You pressed against my chest, melting into my arms, shifting between my legs.

Let us be bundle-tight and launch ourselves to a black foamed universe. My endless fantasies, where I give in to you.

I, ready to bare your loads; willing to lick your wounds.

Phantasm

by Charai Dela

chasing ghosts, that's what it is.
like in dreams of those
long moonlit corridors
where i can't
hear my own steps
and the mirrors just show reflections,
images,
but not what's there.
not me.
not you.
i breathe you
against the surface,
a thing of mist, crystallized smoke.

i am liminal. you live on my threshold.
you haunt me,
hovering on the verge of my vision,
the blind spot
where my brain supplements perception
with what seems fit to make the picture whole.
not with
what's missing.
you are what isn't there,
the immaterial,
the empty space
which makes up
the greater part of solid matter.

the undefined, the blank position, the unknown possibility.
just
as i turn
around
you hit me full force,
torch and dagger and all,
lighting my belly
and the images start spinning and your negative burns on my retina.
whispering endearments
so my breath catches in my throat
from the sudden ache
between my thighs.
the intoxicating scent of myrtle.

you are my spectre
and i conjure you.

Yes

by Roxy Jones

It was you,
soft and pleading,
"Baby,"
in the morning light —
the sight of your warm, pink skin
rising and falling
against the silhouettes of barren black trees.

At the edge of the precipice, my nerves rippling with electricity,
i tumbled down into you,
past mountains of unknown fears
and came to rest against a strong fiery thigh.
"Baby," you purred,
as my tongue sang wicked songs
to your wanton shadows,
fingers groping their way inside,
pressing, reaching, thrusting
leaving me unable to speak except to repeat,
over and over,

"beautiful."

"Beautiful, beautiful love,"
my prayer of thanksgiving, whispered in reverence,
as silent music pulsed through you in waves,
your body danced,

rolling and bucking as your moans became
an opera of pleasure.

Inside you, a part of you,
i held your hand and kissed your chest.
Oh, rapturous woman, lush and deep,
i was waiting all these years for you
and you have blessed me with ecstasy
and stillness
and
the answer to my question.

How could i not have known? The answer had always been

Yes.

Gothic Snare

by Ted D'Leyo

Jack boots, black leather, strength and purpose
Girded by a knotted 'drape noir'

Corset defining the shape beneath
Embroidered colors swirled on black
Bounding a line of silver eyes
And hooks designed to hold
Yet made to be undone

Arms gloved in open nets of black
White throat hung with another net
Wrought of jeweled chain
Draped above
The corsets focal swelling
Of softly rounded breasts

So much a part
Of the snare she's made
To catch the eye
To draw the gaze
And baited with herself
That when it's sprung
She finds her own heart caught

Though words form on her lips
The eloquence is in her eyes
Confessing her soul
Longing to be found
Begging to be freed
Of the very nets that trapped her.

55 Words
by Kimberlykate Neagle

There
On my knees
With all that I am surrendered to you
I am freed.
So Consumed
In you, by you
That I see myself as you see me
More Beautiful
In my suffering
Braver
Than I thought I could be
Bigger
Outside myself
Stronger
Than I would have dreamt
My Only struggle
For grace.

Is Seeking Other

by Kimberlykate Neagle

This was her idea, all of it. She had found him, written the first letter, packed her own bag and got on a plane. So, it wasn't exactly as if she had stumbled into this moment unwittingly. So why then, was she standing in a hotel parking lot wondering if she had lost her mind?

It had just been a little random surfing, hadn't it? Who knew that such a site even existed? In retrospect it made perfect sense, but at the time, she had just been curious.

"Facebook for kinky people?" she said aloud with a giggle. "Oh, I have to see this." Katherine Kennedy, Kate to her friends, poured herself a second glass of pinot noir and clicked "Join."

She started with the pictures. Wide eyed and holding her breath she clicked image after image. The gallery was a pictorial orgy of sadomasochism, temptation and eerie beauty. Women with skin striped red from cane strokes, or intricately bound with rope. There were boys who played as puppies and girls who wanted to be ponies, and Kate thought them all too beautiful.

She found herself drawn back to the site almost nightly, following threads and reading posts, but always as an observer. On the fifth night, she followed a thread someone named DomN8u had started about a photo. There were enough "oohs" and "aahs" and whimpers of envy that she hunted the picture down.

When she finally found it, her breath stopped and her chest ached.

Shot in black and white, the photo was of a girl. She sat nude, save a steel band around her neck, on a wet concrete floor. Her pale skin was discoloured with bruises, her hair tangled, and her delicate face streaked with mascara. She was clinging to the leg of a man only half in frame, caressing the tip of his boot.

She clicked on the photographer's profile. He was handsome, literate, passionate, and frankly, he frightened her. Something in his eyes... in his words... left her a little unsettled... and greatly overheated. Kate wrote to him.

Three months later she was on a plane. That was how she had gotten here.

During the daily emails and frequent calls they had gotten to know one another. Occasionally, she had the odd sensation that he knew her better than she knew herself. She once asked him casually what she should wear on their first date. He had told her that he would send her what she was to wear. A week later she received a box containing a short pale pink skirt, white shirt and a small steel anal plug that had an emerald coloured stone in its base. It had taken her two weeks of practice before she could get the plug in.

She was lost in her own thoughts, distracted by the weight of the plug in her belly, and the cool night air on her legs when his bike rolled to a stop in front of her. He looked at her and Kate was suddenly terrified.

"Oh my God, what am I doing?" Kate thought to herself. "This is real. He is real. This isn't Stephen whatshisname who gave you a couple of spanks in college after too many kamikazes."

He moved toward her, and had it taken him even a moment longer to close the distance between them... she might have run.

He pulled her to his chest and she dissolved into him, her legs unsteady, heart pulsing in her ears. He lifted her face kissing her deeply... holding her until she found her breath.

Without a word, he took her hand in his and led her to the bike. He stopped, placing one hand low on her belly and the other high on her back. Her body stiffened instinctively and he spoke for the first time, "Shhh, it's okay. I'm here now," he whispered in her ear as he massaged the back of her neck. "Are you frightened?"

She looked up at him wide eyed and nodded, her body bow taut.

"Shall I help you be brave?" he asked, still stroking her softly.

She stood silent, watching his face for an eternity, until he released his hand and took a step back from her. The wind stabbed at her neck where his hand had lay, and she knew instantly that the pain of him not touching her would be far more agonizing than anything he could do to her body.

"Yes!" she blurted, "Please?"

He folded his arms across his chest. "Please what?"

She squirmed, dropped her gaze to his boots, "Please help me be brave, Sir."

He stepped toward her again, placing his hands back where they had been and felt her soften. This time she moved with him, planting her palms on the leather seat. He raked his hands down her back, and she arched beneath his touch. He landed a solemn smack on the thin fabric skirt hard enough that it echoed through the parking lot. Kate's knees buckled and she bit down hard on her lip. His hand slid under her skirt and cupped her swollen mound. Her small clit throbbed in his palm and jumped when his thumb slid between her cheeks searching for the emerald coloured jewel.

He stood her up quickly and spun her so that she faced him. Her lips trembled and her eyes were wet with the first of her tears. He wiped a smudge of mascara from her cheek, kissed her softly and helped her onto the bike.

When she settled, he climbed on in front of her, reaching back, taking her arms, pulling her breasts hard into his back. He squeezed her hands then let them rest in his lap. His cock jumped once under the softness of her touch. He tilted his head back until it was lying on her shoulder.

"If you cum on my seat you're going to clean it up," he growled over the thunder of the engine.

The bike jumped hard as it shifted into gear and pulled away from the curb. They swayed from lane to lane as he sped up the onramp and flew down the nearly deserted expressway. The force pulled at her core and ground a low deep moan from her chest... her hair whipped around her face, the ends biting and stinging the tender skin of her throat. Her hand tightened around his cock as they shot between cars and under lights that turned her hair the color of a new penny in the sun.

Tears leaked from the corners of her eyes... this was sensory overload, every part of her body electric and throbbing as the bike rocked beneath her... her swollen clit pulsed against the soft leather of the seat, and she tried... however futilely... to press her legs together and stop the explosion.

He could hear her cry out, even over the wind and noise... feel her body tighten... her hand open and close around his cock. He jacked his left leg down hard and shifted into fourth, watching the speedometer climb... 60... 70... 80. She cried out again.

It could have been minutes or hours... she couldn't tell... when they finally pulled off the road and he parked the bike under a canopy of trees. It was as if she were dreaming... everything so far away, the world completely silent except for her own soft pants.

He got off the bike and watched her for a few moments... then took her hand and urged her from the seat slowly, letting her find her balance. She looked at him through clouded eyes, blinking furiously. He spun her around to face the bike, the sound of traffic playing behind them in the distance.

"Kate....." his voice seemed to float down to her, from some place high. "Kate....." she blinked and he could see her begin to process... see the spell break. "Look at that." He spoke slowly letting the words work their way through the haze. She squinted... her line of sight trailing down his arm, over his extended forefinger to the seat of the bike. She could feel the blood rush to her cheeks and tried to drop her face.

"What did I tell you, Kate? Do you remember?"

She lowered her burning face. "I remember."

She paused a moment, fresh tears threatening to spill, and then gathered her hair over her shoulder. Sticking out her tongue as far as she can… making it long and flat against her chin. Tentatively, she watched him for approval as she lowered her face to the seat and began to drag her tongue across the leather. Intoxicated by her own scent she moved faster, feverishly, almost gagging on the thickness of her own cum… its sticky sweetness.

He stepped behind her, "Lift your skirt and offer yourself to me."

She did as he asked, and she sobbed as he took her.

Two days later she was on another plane, a band of steel locked around her neck, long skirt to hide the cane marks on her thighs, and the epic realization that her life would never… ever… be the same.

Ripe

by Tito Titus

I have been here before
naked beneath this tree
this very tree!
ochre lichen, rough bark
on a bright hot day
standing in grass waist high
and yellowed by summer
with two naked women
and a hard on
picking luscious plums,
juice running down my chin.
They smiled sweetly
speaking softly of harvest
embracing their fruit.

What Is Butch?

by Roxy Jones

Butch is that red-and-white, candy-striped, aftershave-and-razor hair cut, the hand you wish you dared reach out to feel those strong, ripped shoulders, that neck that slides up, close-cropped, under the fabric, like she was born with that cap on, like they were made for each other, lookin out at the world like it's one big fight or maybe just last night's lay. The way she shines those boots that have known the ground, walked miles outside this town, out of her house and never looking back, marching and dancing with her girl, but always easy, hips that were built to press up close when her girl sways and leans her head back, stretching out her neck, long and graceful, inviting her inside.

It's the jeans that leave a little, or a lot, to the imagination, but never tell their secrets, like a well-worn friend, with a belt thicker than your arm shoved through the loops and a buckle from mom on Christmas that says "I get it." It's the bulge of a brown leather wallet in the back that's been shined with every step in those ground-knowing boots, the one that fits the shape of that damn sexy ass almost as well as her girlfriend's eager hand. It's the pocket knife that waits at the ready, heavy in her hand and full of power, the shiny chrome chain that hangs down like a challenge, the flask of tequila on her hip, the old pocket watch that used to belong to somebody's grandpa, the plaid/flannel/seersucker/denim/tweed that says, "no, I meant to look like this" as she walks down the street projecting hard-won courage, meeting gaze for gaze, never missing a step.

It's that hard leather jacket, pulled up with a shrug and zipped up tight to hold in her shape, that zipper that lets your mind wander to what's hidden underneath, not just a guy, but something beautiful and dangerous all wrapped up in gasp-with-your-mouth-open handsome. It's a steady hand, that practiced lean, the wink that melts you, those arms that can hold a soccer ball or a baby with the same tenderness and strength, that subtle nod of recognition in a passing crowd. It's the mouse-catching, spider-moving, shelf-building, oil-changing young James Dean that blushes with pride when his girl asks him to pick up tampons at the store. It's the strong arm around your shoulders and the warm, sure chest when the night is dark and the walk home is long and cold. It's a thousand brave acts that challenge the world to keep up, to see what's right in front of them. It's a swagger, an affront, a tribute and, at the end of the day, a drink with the guys in that little corner bar that's no bigger than a postage stamp, where the beer is cheap and the company is certain.

It's a look and I'm gone, baby, gone, a growl in my belly, a second and third and forth glance back because I can't keep my eyes off you hunger that I can't deny. It's that attitude that gets my attention, and the grin that knocks me to my knees. It's the most beautiful sight in the whole damn world and everything that I've ever wanted. It's the butterflies in my gut, the thanksgiving prayer to god, and the shy smile I can't help when I say hello.

It's butch, and I'm thankful every day of my life that you were born to be that way.

pink and devastating (part 1)
by Jen Cross

(inspired by "we met at the corner of..." – Thea Hillman)

I know what you've heard: gossip thronged around the edges of the community, snatches here and there. You heard that Zora took me down, that I let her shove her hand up in my aching, pearly pink. But, baby, before we go any further tonight, I gotta set the record straight.

We met at the corner of pink and devastating, each of us trying to high highest femme the whole room, me in flounce-y, spangled, peppermint-stripe tutu, stacked platform lace-up ballet shoes, a ruffled top split wide down the front, tied at the midriff, and hair sprayed within an inch of its life with Aqua Net and Pink Neon Manic Panic. Oh, and no panties. And her with that fat fluffy rose boa, first of all, which was so long that it trailed on the ground behind her even as she made her way through the tight throng of the dressed (both over- and under-) at this year's Drag King contest, in 4-inch high spike heel Lucite pink puma peep toes, a matching long skirt that flung itself from her waist down to just above her ankles and cleaved itself down along one side to reveal her too goddamn perfect plump (and glitter-sheened!) calves and thighs — the rose-paisley bustier, the thick dark hair in a cloisonné upsweep held together by cherry blossom chopsticks, a couple of combs, and, yes, spit and prayers — oh, and no panties — there was no keeping from setting it off. I dropped my butch escort's arm as soon as Miz Pristine made her entrance, needing all of my energy to lance through the fauxhawks and thrift store finery, plumage and socks stuffed in varying nether regions in order to um make her *acquaintance*. I meant to demand some sort of tithe from her, this new-come-to-town trying to defame my own throne of highest femme in the land.

She just stood so you'd think she'd come to attention (but I saw, didn't you, that she came to be attended to) pursed her MAC bright lips together and lowered her impossibly long, impossibly fake, impossibly PERFECT Too Wong Foo Priscilla drag queen lashes just to half mast, shifted so that slit in her skirt shut the door on my wandering eye, focusing my attention, you could say, reminding me that, yes, I had been an adoring young butch once, too and she put that long tongue out just a little a shade, you could say purplish rose lacquered lips split by school-perfect pink eraser muscle and she lit a new shine to her lips and all of mine then and there, thank you and she said, "Ooh, girl, look at those shoes."

She grinned, wide, then shadowed in, pinpointing her meaning, she said: "So stable."

She cocked one hip, 'cause it was meant to be cocked that way, popping out into and claiming more of the space that the crowd had cleared for this collision of femme dominion.

Now, some say that plain platforms, a solid chunky fat heel, is cheating when it comes to the way girls do with each other. Some say if it's not spiked it's practically flats. Maybe she was in this category. I can't say as I could tell you. Maybe she was dishing some evil shade. But let me tell you, honey, that place where my panties ought to have covered had my parents raised even a halfway proper lady was running thick with all the possibilities and I stood firm, legs spread just enough, and pelvis cocked forward, sure, and could not be jostled by the crowd and I said, "I bet you want to find out, don't you?"

Her cheeks went a red that clashed with her outfit and I checked myself a pointing the femme register in the sky 'cause even though I know about the inherent wrong of girl on girl competition sometimes you just gotta win one for the home team, don't you? But really, I just wanted to keep the redness coming into those taupe cheeks.

Lord, what was coming over me? I *wanted her,* in that split skirt, picturing split thighs, all right, yes, over my big brawny girl shoulders, all of our tits at attention while I rock in and out of her purple pink lower lips, the very hot red rose fat baby boy cock that I carried in my bag, already ready, I came to realize, to be strapped not around some one of these king-y wanna-bes but instead around my meaty thighs.

Now, boys, take a picture of this 'cause it's never happened before and it's not likely to come again. It's well known that I am not just a pillow queen: I am an empress. After a few years topping bioboys after I started having sex as a teenager, I met an old-school butch during my first excursion to my small home town's dyke bar. The first time I laid my eyes on her I laid down. I mean, when she laid her hands on me, I fell so hard on my back that the sky started crying. There are better metaphors than that. *I* started crying—but only after I wore that butch out. The only time I'm not on my back is when I'm on my knees. It's not just do-me, it's do away with any ideas you might have had about getting done. My pussy's so pillowy hard and fine, there are butches still lost down there, exploring and seeking and navigating all that good terrain.

Now Miss Pristine—or Zora is how she was called by other people but I liked to call her Pristine 'cause she was always put together like a shiny piece of plastic and she hated any kind of mess. I was shocked as hell to see her out at the Drag King contest, which was held at a warehouse apace in the not-yet-completely-gentrified part of way downtown and had a concrete floor already coated with beer drippings, sweat and mud. It was clustery hot and barely ventilated, so most of the girls start melting immediately after setting one manicured foot into the door (boys, too, if they hadn't put their spirit gum on just right; there were dropping moustaches and sliding soul patches all through the room). And the only time Miss P utters the words *Do me* is after she's fucked some tender butch bottom til ze's wrung all the way out and just wetting up again, and Miss P's finally ready to come herself. The way the story goes, she sets herself up in her tall throne, parts her legs (high heeled shoes pushing her arches and calves into a more pornographic roundness than anyone might think possible), points one short-nailed perfectly polished index finger at her pussy, and the butch is to get her off with no more than thirty strokes on her clit. (This count is well confirmed.) The ones who try to insert anything whatsoever into Zora's soaking slit are summarily dismissed — they hear the buzzing and the "oh! Oh! Oh!"s before they hit the front door. Miss P might get a little mussed while she's fucking someone (though no one knew her not to use gloves), a soft sheen of sweat might break across her brow, a cleft of hair might fall lose from her coif, but no one would ever say they'd seen her *disheveled.*

So it was not an idle thing I said there, insinuating that she might have been complimenting the stability of my footwear because she imagined me in a position compromising in more ways than one. Zora just wrinkled her long nose at me, barely a sniff, let her eyes fall on the door to the back stage side entrance and then didn't she just turn and part the crowd without a word.

The things I did, now, I did because of her. People need to know that part. I mean, I saw her look at that side stage door before turning away and forcing me to watch her ass switch switch switch into the congealed crowd before all the faces of our own personal audience had turned back to snatch their eyes to me, to see what I was going to do now, now that she had left me and my question just *hanging* here. I mean, sure, I still throbbed like a woofer at a bad 90s dyke club still I was beginning to smell my own goddamn cunt over and above the accumulated aromas of second-hand smoke and cheap-ass cologne. I worked my jaw like I was popping gum, even though my mouth was suddenly too empty and dry, and said, "Figures," then pursed my lips and turned my own self around, pushing between two thrift-store-suit-jacketed tranny boys behind me, wiggling out of any ideas they were forming about putting me in the middle of their T-dance sandwich. I made a beeline for the bathrooms, shoved my way through the clouds of glitter and hairspray into an empty stall, locked the door and sat my shaking self down. I didn't stop to think—not on your life. I popped open the clasp of my bag and took out the nylon harness that I carry out with me to these sorts of events (so as to foreswear that sad butch song, "oh I didn't plan on getting it on tonight I'm not packing la la la." You know how it goes—I don't even have to hum any bars). I settled the harness around my thighs and ass, then fitted in my Ms. Big Red, tucked her in place under the tutu ruffles and waistband, and felt something else in me thicken and harden. Maybe it was my resolve. I didn't dare touch myself, just pissed, patted dry, straightened up and shoved back out into the crowd.

Thoughts to Myself

by Raina Johnson

As I leave you,
everything I wear smells like your mouth
and your skin-
leftovers I cannot wait to get back home to devour:
hide away in a closet and lick at my own flesh,
pull at my own hair,
taste more of you sliding further down my throat.
But, for now,
riding on this nearly empty boat to home,
your flavor and fever move like a whirlpool
through my senses.
Oh, how my lip throbs,
where the wound you gifted me
screams to strangers
who eye it curiously:
"Did he beat her?"
Or
"Did she bite it?"
I touch it with my finger;
tap, tap, tapping it.
I stare out the window
wondering why you left your mark
on something that you do not possess.
and wonder why
I long to keep it there

www.ingramcontent.com/pod-product-compliance
Ingram Content Group UK Ltd.
Pitfield, Milton Keynes, MK11 3LW, UK
UKHW041926190726
13854UKWH00003B/1476